THE RED SHOES

BY HANS CHRISTIAN ANDERSEN

Golden Age of Illustration Series

POOK PRESS

Copyright © 2015 Pook Press
An imprint of Read Publishing Ltd.

Home Farm, 44 Evesham Road, Cookhill, Alcester,
Warwickshire, B49 5LJ

British Library Cataloguing-in-Publication Data.
A catalogue record for this book is available from
the British Library.

www.pookpress.co.uk

CONTENTS

LIST OF ILLUSTRATIONS

Biography

of

HANS CHRISTIAN ANDERSEN

"First, you undergo such a terrible amount of suffering,
and then you become famous."

This quote, taken from Hans Christian Andersen's autobiography *The Fairy Tale of My Life* (1855), could serve as a one-sentence biography of the great writer. Before he achieved global fame as an author of children's literature on a par with Aesop and the Brothers Grimm, Andersen suffered three decades of toil, isolation and strife. Had it not been for his unwavering determination to become a professional writer, the literary realm may never have been gifted tales such now-timeless as 'The Little Mermaid', 'The Emperor's New Clothes' and 'The Ugly Duckling'.

*

Born in Odense, the third largest city in Denmark, on Tuesday 2nd April 1805, Andersen was the only son of a sickly, 22-year old shoemaker and his older wife. His family were virtually penniless, and Andersen grew up in a one-bedroom house in Odense's poorest quarter. In his youth, he attended school sporadically, and spent far more time memorizing and reciting stories than studying in any traditional fashion. This propensity for storytelling, combined with the sudden death of his father in 1816, led to Andersen's mother deciding her eleven-year son needed to learn a proper, wage-paying trade. She sent him to apprentice as a weaver, after which he worked reluctantly in a tobacco factory and a tailor's shop.

In 1819, aged fourteen, Andersen travelled a hundred miles to the Danish capital Copenhagen to seek his fortune. However, his first three years were marked by extreme poverty and a string of failed financial endeavours. At first, having an excellent soprano voice, Andersen was accepted into a boy's choir, but when his voice began to break he was forced to quit. He then attempted to become a ballet dancer, but his tall, gangly body prevented him from finding any success. In desperation, Andersen even attempted manual labour – a style of work to which he had never been suited. During these three years, following advice given him by a poet he had met while singing in the choir, Andersen began to write, penning a number of short stories and poems.

In 1822, at the age of 17, Andersen's dogged persistence paid off, following a chance encounter with a man named Jonas Collin. Collin was director of the Royal Danish Theatre, and having read a number of Andersen's writings – including his first published story, 'The Ghost at Palnatoke's Grave' – felt convinced he showed promise. Collin approached King Frederik VI (1768-1839), and managed to convince the monarch to partially fund the young artist's education. (In recent times, various other theories pertaining to Andersen's royal connection have arisen, stemming from both

Andersen's father's firm belief that he possessed noble heritage, and the notion that Andersen himself may have been an illegitimate son of the royal family.)

Andersen began his education in the towns of Slagelse and Helsingor, on the Danish island of Zealand. However, despite receiving the finest schooling, he was an average student – possibly because he suffered from dyslexia – and was mocked by other pupils for his desire to become a writer. At one point, he lived at his schoolmaster's home, where he was physically abused. Andersen would later describe his time in school as the most unhappy period of his life. In 1827, his despair led Jonas Collin to remove him from school, and organise for Andersen to complete his studies in Copenhagen with a private teacher. In 1828, the 23-year old passed the required exams for entrance into the University of Copenhagen.

In 1829, during his first year of university studies, Andersen achieved his first notable literary success with a short story entitled 'A Journey on Foot from Holmen's Canal to the East Point of Amager'. During the same semester, he published a comedy and a collection of poems. Four years later, Andersen received a grant from King Frederik for travel expenses, and spent the next 18 months roaming through Germany, Switzerland, France and Italy – the last of which he was deeply fond. For Andersen, this trip began a lifelong infatuation with travel – over the course of his life he would embark on some thirty extended journeys, spending a combined fifteen years of his life in other countries. Indeed, aside from the fairy tales that would eventually cement his fame, Andersen was renowned for his vivid travelogues, and is credited with having declared "to travel is to live."

In 1835, Andersen published his breakthrough piece of writing – an autobiographical novel titled *The Improvisatore*. An instant success, the book's detailing of rural Italy delighted readers all across Europe, and it was translated into French and German within two years of its publication. Also in 1835, Andersen published the first of his now-legendary fairy tales. Despite their modern status, these first efforts weren't immediate successes, being overshadowed by his next two novels, *O.T.* (1836) and *Only a Fiddler* (1837), and his *Scandinavianist* poem *I am a Scandinavian* (1840).

The fame of Andersen's fairy tales (revolutionary in the field of Danish children's literature) began to grow during the late thirties. Between 1835 and 1837, over three booklets, he published his first collection of stories, which included 'The Tinderbox', 'The Princess and the Pea', 'Thumbelina', 'The Little Mermaid', and 'The Emperor's New Clothes'. In 1838, he published his second series, *Fairy Tales Told for Children,* which consisted of 'The Daisy', well-known tale 'The Steadfast Tin Soldier' and 'The Wild Swans'. Over the next seven years, Andersen continued to regularly publish collections, the 1843 version of which included 'The Ugly Duckling' – cementing his reputation as a leading author of children's literature. Over the rest of his life, Andersen would go on to publish a total of more than a hundred and fifty fairy tales.

In 1838, the spectre of poverty was banished from Andersen's life forever, when King Frederick VI awarded him an annual stipend for life. By the 1840s, he was an internationally renowned author, celebrated across the continent for his apparently inimitable storytelling gift. During visits to Germany and England in 1846 and 1847 respectively, he was hailed as a foreign dignitary, and while in London he met Charles Dickens for the first time, returning some ten years later to stay at the writers' home for five years. In 1846, he received the Knighthood of the Red Eagle from King Friedrich Wilhelm IV of Prussia, and while in France he spent time with a number of famous artists, including Honore de Balzac, Alexandre Dumas and Victor Hugo. (Interestingly, however, in his native Denmark, the praise for Andersen's work wasn't quite so unanimous. Amongst others, the philosopher Søren Kierkegaard attacked his work for being naïve and fundamentally vacuous.)

Andersen spent many of the later years of his life penning well-received travelogues, including his acclaimed *Pictures of Sweden* (1851) and *In Spain* (1863). Meanwhile, despite a desire to build his literary reputation on more adult fiction, his *Fairy Tales* continued to appear in instalments, and to prove extremely popular with readers. The last batch appeared in the spring of 1872, a few weeks before Andersen fell out of bed and severely injured himself. Over the next couple of years, Andersen's literary output declined, and he developed liver cancer. He died on the 4th August 1875, while in the care of his friends in Copenhagen.

*

It is perhaps curious that a man who never married, and who never had any children of his own, managed to pen tales so well-tuned to the child psyche. Part of the explanation for this may lay in Andersen's own troubled life. For one, the Dane was denied anything like a proper childhood of his own, with his father dying when he just eleven and his mother forcing him into the world of manual work. Also, Andersen had an odd and in many ways childlike relationship with love and lust. A lifelong celibate, he frequently fell in love with unattainable women – his tale 'The Nightingale' was inspired by Andersen's unrequited love for opera singer Jenny Lind – and also experienced a number of unreciprocated passions for various men in his life. (Tales such as 'The Little Mermaid' and 'The Ugly Duckling' play deeply into themes of impossible love and poor self-image.) This self-imposed celibacy, combined with his apparently impassioned bisexuality, has caused much debate amongst Andersen's biographers. In 2011, a proposal by a number of Danish MPs to instigate a gay pride week in honour of the cherished national poet polarised national opinion.

As an interesting aside, it is worth noting that many of the popular English translations of Andersen's tales are said to lose much of the deeper – and, in many instances, darker – layers that they possess in the original Danish. The original tales are run through with existential and often pained themes; however, during the 1840s, many of Andersen's earliest translators simplified the language and bent the tales to suit strict Victorian ideals of moralism and civility, even going so far as to drastically alter features of the plot. It was due in large part to this that, in

Britain, Andersen's tales came to be viewed as simple, sentimental children's yarns – whereas on the continent they were viewed as much more complex pieces of work. As Andersen himself once stated, in talking about his creative process:

> I seize on an idea for grown-ups, and then tell the story
> to the little ones while always remembering that
> Father and Mother often listen, and you must also
> give them something for their minds.

Later, he complained about the reputation his work had garnered in Britain:

> I said loud and clear that I was dissatisfied...
> that my tales were just as much for older
> people as for children, who only understood
> the outer trappings and did not comprehend
> and take in the whole work until they were mature.

Ultimately, Andersen's tales – originally laced with comedy, social critique, satire and philosophy – have undoubtedly suffered, across various translations and adaptations, from a century and a half of emotional child-proofing. Indeed, no two pieces of work are more guilty of sanitising and sweetening Andersen's life and work than the sugary 1952 biopic *Hans Christian Andersen* and Disney's famous *The Little Mermaid* (1989) – which swapped Andersen's original ending (as contained in this collection) for one in which Ariel and Eric marry and live happily ever after.

However., the original tales, as contained here, remain stunning pieces of fantastic literature. Whatever the facts of Andersen's psychology and sexuality, and regardless of the existence of less-than-satisfactory translations, there is no doubt that Dane ranks with Aesop and the Brothers Grimm as one of the greatest authors of children's literature of all time. His stories have been translated into more than 150 languages – from Inupiat in the Arctic to Swahili in Africa – and have inspired almost countless adaptations (including as theme parks, in both Japan and China). "The Emperor's New Clothes" and "The Ugly Duckling" have both passed into the English language as well-known idioms, and. International Children's Book Day has been celebrated on the 2nd April – Andersen's birthday – since 1967.

Ultimately, however much he might have wanted to be taken more seriously as a writer of adult fiction, Andersen had an exceptional, mercurial relationship with his child readers; a relationship which lasted right up until the weeks before his passing, when he informed the composer writing the music for his funeral that "most of the people who will walk after me will be children, so make the beat keep time with little steps."

* * *

'The Red Shoes' was first published in April of 1845, as part of Andersen's *New Fairy Tales: First Volume, Third Collection*. Andersen explained the source of the story as being an incident he had witnessed as a small child. His father, he stated, had been sent a piece of red silk by a rich lady, who wanted the material converted into a pair of dancing slippers. Andersen's father produced the slippers, but the rich woman was horrified at the result, and in reaction to her harsh criticism, he cut the shoes up in front of her.

'The Red Shoes' has been adapted a number of times across across various media. In 2005, it inspired a Korean horror film, and more recently it has been adapted by an arts collective in Austin Texas into a cirque noir aerial ballet.

M. M. Owen

Introduction

to

THE GOLDEN AGE OF ILLUSTRATION

The 'Golden age of Illustration' refers to a period customarily defined as lasting from the latter quarter of the nineteenth century until just after the First World War. In this period of no more than fifty years the popularity, abundance and most importantly the unprecedented upsurge in quality of illustrated works marked an astounding change in the way that publishers, artists and the general public came to view this hitherto insufficiently esteemed art form.

Until the latter part of the nineteenth century, the work of illustrators was largely proffered anonymously, and in England it was only after Thomas Bewick's pioneering technical advances in wood engraving that it became common to acknowledge the artistic and technical expertise of book and magazine illustrators. Although widely regarded as the patriarch of the *Golden Age*, Walter Crane (1845-1915) started his career as an anonymous illustrator – gradually building his reputation through striking designs, famous for their sharp outlines and flat tints of colour. Like many other great illustrators to follow, Crane operated within many different mediums; a lifelong disciple of William Morris and a member of the Arts and Crafts Movement, he designed all manner of objects including wallpaper, furniture, ceramic ware and even whole interiors. This incredibly important and inclusive phase of British design proved to have a lasting impact on illustration both in the United Kingdom and Europe as well as America.

The artists involved in the Arts and Crafts Movement attempted to counter the ever intruding Industrial Revolution (the first wave of which lasted roughly from 1750-1850) by bringing the values of beautiful and inventive craftsmanship back into the sphere of everyday life. It must be noted that around the turn of the century the boundaries between what would today be termed 'fine art' as opposed to 'crafts' and 'design' were far more fluid and in many cases non-operational, and many illustrators had lucrative painterly careers in addition to their design work. The Romanticism of the *Pre Raphaelite Brotherhood* combined with the intricate curvatures of the *Art Nouveaux* movement provided influential strands running through most illustrators work. The latter especially so for the Scottish illustrator Anne Anderson (1874-1930) as well as the Dutch artist Kay Nielson (1886-1957), who was also inspired by the stunning work of Japanese artists such as Hiroshige.

One of the main accomplishments of nineteenth century illustration lay in its ability to reach far wider numbers than the traditional 'high arts'. In 1892 the American critic William A. Coffin praised the new medium for popularising art; 'more has been done through the medium of illustrated literature... to make the masses of people realise that there is such a thing as art and that it is worth caring about'. Commercially, illustrated publications reached their zenith with the burgeoning 'Gift Book' industry which emerged in the first decade of the twentieth century. The first widely distributed gift book was published in 1905. It comprised of Washington Irving's short story *Rip Van Winkle* with the addition of 51 colour plates by a true master of illustration; Arthur Rackham. Rackham created each plate by first painstakingly drawing his subject in a sinuous pencil line before applying an ink layer – then he used layer upon layer of delicate watercolours to build up the romantic yet calmly ethereal results on which his reputation was constructed. Although Rackham is now one of the most recognisable names in illustration, his delicate palette owed no small debt to Kate Greenaway (1846-1901) – one of the first female illustrators whose pioneering and incredibly subtle use of the watercolour medium resulted in her election to the Royal Institute of Painters in Water Colours in 1889.

The year before Arthur Rackam's illustrations for *Rip Van Winkle* were published, a young and aspiring French artist by the name of Edmund Dulac (1882-1953) came to London and was to create a similarly impressive legacy. His timing could not have been more fortuitous. Several factors converged around the turn of the century which allowed illustrators and publishers alike a far greater freedom of creativity than previously imagined. The origination of the 'colour separation' practice meant that colour images, extremely faithful to the original artwork could be produced on a grand scale. Dulac possessed a rigorously painterly background (more so than his contemporaries) and was hence able to utilise the new technology so as to allow the colour itself to refine and define an object as opposed to the traditional pen and ink line. It has been estimated that in 1876 there was only one 'colour separation' firm in London, but by 1900 this number had rocketed to fifty. This improvement in printing quality also meant a reduction in labour, and coupled with the introduction of new presses and low-cost supplies of paper this meant that publishers could for the first time afford to pay high wages for highly talented artists.

Whilst still in the U.K, no survey of the *Golden Age of Illustration* would be complete without a mention of the Heath-Robinson brothers. Charles Robinson was renowned for his beautifully detached style, whether in pen and ink or sumptuous watercolours. Whilst William (the youngest) was to later garner immense fame for his carefully constructed yet tortuous machines operated by comical, intensely serious attendants. After World War One the Robinson brothers numbered among the few artists of the Golden Age who continued to regularly produce illustrated works. As we move towards the United States, one illustrator - Howard Pyle (1853-1911) stood head and shoulders above his contemporaries as the most distinguished illustrator of the age. From 1880 onwards Pyle illustrated over 100 volumes, yet it was not quantity which ensured his precedence over other American (and European) illustrators, but quality.

Pyle's sumptuous illustrations benefitted from a meticulous composition process livened with rich colour and deep recesses, providing a visual framework in which tales such as *Robin Hood* and *The Four Volumes of the Arthurian Cycle* could come to life. These are publications which remain continuous good sellers up till the present day. His flair and originality combined with a thoroughness of planning and execution were principles which he passed onto his many pupils at the *Drexel Institute of Arts and Sciences*. Two such pupils were Jessie Willcox Smith (1863-1935) who went on to illustrate books such as *The Water Babies* and *At the Back of North Wind* and perhaps most famously Maxfield Parrish (1870-1966) who became famed for luxurious colour (most remarkably demonstrated in his blue paintings) and imaginative designs; practices in no short measure gleaned from his tutor. As an indication of Parrish's popularity, in 1925 it was estimated that one fifth of American households possessed a Parrish reproduction.

As is evident from this brief introduction to the 'Golden Age of Illustration', it was a period of massive technological change and artistic ingenuity. The legacy of this enormously important epoch lives on in the present day – in the continuing popularity and respect afforded to illustrators, graphic and fine artists alike. The ensuing volumes provide a fascinating insight into an era of intense historical and creative development, bringing out of print books and their art back to life for both young and old to revel and delight in.

We hope that the current reader adores these books as much as we do. Enjoy.

Amelia Carruthers

Karen.

THE RED SHOES

There was once a little girl, very pretty and delicate, but so poor that in summer-time she always went barefoot, and in winter wore large wooden shoes, so that her little ankles grew quite red and sore.

In the village dwelt the shoemaker's mother. She sat down one day and made out of some old pieces of red cloth a pair of little shoes; they were clumsy enough, certainly, but they fitted the little girl tolerably well, and she gave them to her. The little girl's name was Karen.

She sat down one day and made out of some old pieces
of red cloth, a pair of little shoes.

It was the day of her mother's funeral when the red shoes were given to Karen; they were not at all suitable for mourning, but she had no others, and in them she walked with bare legs behind the miserable straw bier.

Just then a large old carriage rolled by; in it sat a large old lady, who looked at the little girl and pitied her, and said to the priest, "Give me the little girl and I will take care of her."

Karen thought it was all for the sake of the red shoes that the old lady had taken this fancy to her; but the old lady said they were frightful, and they were burned. And Karen was dressed very neatly; she was taught to read and to work; and people told her she was pretty. But the mirror said, "Thou art more than pretty, thou art beautiful!"

It happened one day that the Queen travelled through that part of the country with her little daughter, the Princess; and all the people, Karen amongst them, crowded in front of the palace, whilst the little Princess stood, dressed in white, at a window, for every one to see her. She wore neither train nor gold crown; but on her feet were pretty red morocco shoes–much prettier ones, indeed, than those the shoemaker's mother had made for little Karen. Nothing in the world could be compared to these red shoes!

Karen was now old enough to be confirmed; she was to have both new frock and new shoes. The rich shoemaker in the town took the measure of her little foot. Large glass cases full of neat shoes and shining boots were fixed round the room; however, the old lady's sight was not very good, and, naturally enough, she had not so much pleasure in looking at them as Karen had. Amongst the shoes was a pair of red ones, just like those worn by the Princess. How gay they were! And the shoemaker said they had been made for a count's daughter, but had not quite fitted her.

"They are of polished leather," said the old lady; "see how they shine!"

"Yes, they shine beautifully!" exclaimed Karen. And, as the shoes fitted her, they were bought; but the old lady did not know that they were red, for she would never have suffered Karen to go to confirmation in red shoes. But Karen did so.

Everybody looked at her feet, and, as she walked up the nave to the chancel, it seemed to her that even the antique sculptured figures on the monuments, with their stiff ruffs and long black robes, fixed their eyes on her red shoes. Of them only she thought when the Bishop laid his hand on her head, when he spoke of Holy Baptism, of her covenant with God, and how that she must now be a full-grown Christian. The organ sent forth its deep, solemn tones, the children's sweet voices mingled with those of the choristers, but Karen still thought only of her red shoes.

That afternoon, when the old lady was told that Karen had worn red shoes at her confirmation, she was much vexed, and told Karen that they were quite unsuitable; and that, henceforward, whenever she went to church, she must wear black shoes, were they ever so old.

Next Sunday was the communion day. Karen looked first at the red shoes, then at the black ones, then at the red again, and–put them on.

It was beautiful sunshiny weather; Karen and the old lady walked to church through the cornfields; the path was very dusty.

At the church door stood an old soldier; he was leaning on crutches, and had a marvellously long beard, not white, but reddish-hued; and he bowed almost to the earth, and asked the old lady if he might wipe the dust off her shoes. And Karen put out her little foot also. "Oh, what pretty dancing-shoes!" quoth the old soldier; "take care, and mind you do not let them slip off when you dance;" and he passed his hands over them.

The old lady gave the soldier a halfpenny, and then went with Karen into church.

And every one looked at Karen's red shoes, and all the carved figures, too, bent their gaze upon them; and when Karen knelt before the altar, the red shoes still floated before her eyes; she thought of them and of them only; and she forgot to join in the hymn of praise–she forgot to repeat "Our Father."

At last all the people came out of church, and the old lady got into her carriage, Karen was just lifting her foot to follow her, when the old soldier standing in the porch exclaimed, "Only look, what pretty dancing shoes!"

And Karen could not help it; she felt she must make a few of her dancing steps; and after she had once begun, her feet continued to move, just as if the shoes had received power over them: she danced round the churchyard, she could not stop.

The coachman was obliged to run after her; he took hold of her and lifted her into the carriage, but the feet still continued to dance, so as to kick the good old lady most cruelly. At last the shoes were taken off, and the feet had rest.

The coachman was obliged to run behind her.

And now the shoes were put away in a press, but Karen could not help going to look at them every now and then.

The old lady lay ill in bed; the doctor said she could not live much longer. She certainly needed careful nursing, and who should be her nurse and constant attendant but Karen?

But there was to be a grand ball in the town, and Karen was invited; she looked at the old lady who was almost dying–she looked at the red shoes–she put them on, there could be no harm in doing that, at least; she went to the ball, and began to dance.

But, when she wanted to move to the right, the shoes bore her to the left; and, when she would dance up the room, the shoes danced down the room, danced down the stairs, through the streets, and through the gates of the town. Dance she did, and dance she must, straight out into the dark wood.

THE RED SHOES

Away she danced, and away she had to dance right away into the dark forest.

Something all at once shone through the trees. She thought at first it must be the moon's bright face, shining blood-red through the night mists; but no, it was the old soldier with the red beard. He sat there, nodding at her, and repeating, "Only look, what pretty dancing-shoes!"

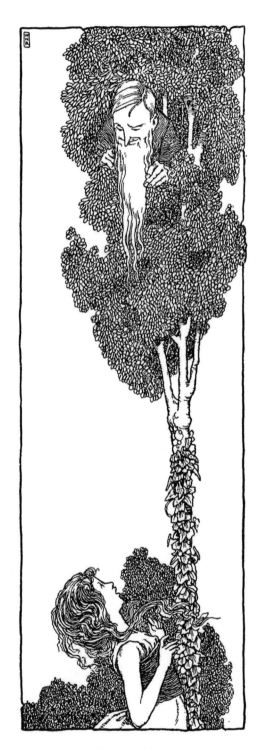

He sat there nodding at her.

See what pretty dancing pumps.

THE · RED · SHOES

She was very much frightened, and tried to throw off her red shoes, but could not unclasp them. She hastily tore off her stockings, but the shoes she could not get rid of–they had, it seemed, grown on to her feet. Dance she did, and dance she must, over field and meadow, in rain and in sunshine, by night and by day.

She wanted to sit down on a pauper's grave where the bitter wormwood grew.

By night!
that was most
horrible! She
danced into the
lonely churchyard,
but the dead there
danced not; they were
at rest. She would
fain have sat down on
the poor man's grave,
where the bitter tansy
grew, but for her there
was neither rest nor
respite. She danced past
the open church door;
there she saw an angel, clad
in long white robes, and
with wings that reached from
his shoulders to the earth; his
countenance was grave and
stern, and in his hand he held
a broad, glittering sword.

"Dance thou shalt," said he; "dance on, in thy red shoes, till thou art pale and cold, and thy skin shrinks and crumples up like a skeleton's! Dance thou shalt still, from door to door, and wherever proud, vain children live thou shalt knock, so that they may hear thee and fear! Dance shalt thou, dance on—"

She danced past the open church door.

She danced, and could not help dancing.

"Mercy!" cried Karen; but she heard not the angel's answer, for the shoes carried her through the gate into the fields, along highways and byways, and still she must dance.

One morning she danced past a door she knew well; she heard psalm-singing from within, and presently a coffin, strewn with flowers, was borne out. Then Karen knew that the good old lady was dead; and she felt herself a thing forsaken by all mankind, and accursed by the Angel of God.

Dance she did, and dance she must, even through the dark night; the shoes bore her continually over thorns and briers, till her limbs were torn and bleeding. Away she danced over the heath to a little solitary house; she knew that the headsman dwelt there, and she tapped with her fingers against the panes, crying–

"Come out! come out! I cannot come in to you, I am dancing."

And the headsman replied, "Surely thou knowest not who I am. I cut off the heads of wicked men, and my axe is very sharp and keen."

"Cut not off my head!" said Karen; "for then I could not live to repent of my sin; but cut off my feet with the red shoes."

And then she confessed to him all her sin, and the headsman cut off her feet with the red shoes on them; but even after this the shoes still danced away with those little feet over the fields, and into the deep forests.

You know who I am? I chop the bad people's heads off,
and I see that my axe is quivering.

And the headsman made her a pair of wooden feet, and hewed down some boughs to serve her as crutches; and he taught her the psalm which is always repeated by criminals; and she kissed the hand that had guided the axe, and went her way over the heath.

"Now, I have certainly suffered quite enough through the red shoes," thought Karen; "I will go to church and let people see me once more I" and she went as fast as she could to the church-porch; but, as she approached it, the red shoes danced before her, and she was frightened, and turned her back.

All that week through she endured the keenest anguish, and shed many bitter tears. However, when Sunday came, she said to herself, "Well, I must have suffered and striven enough by this time; I dare say I am quite as good as many of those who are holding their heads so high in church."

So she took courage and went there; but she had not passed the churchyard gate before she saw the red shoes again dancing before her, and in great terror she again turned back, and more deeply than ever bewailed her sin.

She then went to the pastor's house, and begged that some employment might be given her, promising to work hard and do all she could. She did not wish for any wages, she said; she only wanted a roof to shelter her, and to dwell with good people. And the pastor's wife had pity on her, and took her into her service. And Karen was grateful and industrious.

Every evening she sat silently listening to the pastor, while he read the Holy Scriptures aloud. All the children loved her; but when she heard them talk about dress and finery, and about being as beautiful as a queen, she would sorrowfully shake her head.

Again Sunday came; all the pastor's household went to church, and they asked her if she would not go too, but she sighed and looked, with tears in her eyes, upon her crutches.

When they were all gone, she went into her own little, lowly chamber –it was but just large enough to contain a bed and chair– and there she sat down with her psalm-book in her hand; and while she was meekly and devoutly reading in it, the wind wafted the tones of the organ from the church into her room, and she lifted up her face to heaven and prayed, with tears, "O God, help me!"

Then the sun shone brightly, so brightly–and behold! close before her stood the white-robed Angel of God, the same whom she had seen on that night of horror at the church-porch, but his hand wielded not now, as then, a sharp, threatening sword. He held a lovely green bough, full of roses.

Her soul flew with the sunshine to heaven and no
one there asked about the red shoes.

With this he touched the ceiling, which immediately rose to a great height, a bright gold star spangling in the spot where the Angel's green bough had touched it. And he touched the walls, upon which the room widened, and Karen saw the organ, the old monuments, and the people all sitting in their richly-carved seats, and singing from their psalm-books.

For the church had come home to the poor girl in her narrow chamber, or rather the chamber had grown, as it were, into the church; she sat with the rest of the pastor's household, and, when the psalm was ended, they looked up and nodded to her, saying, "Thou didst well to come, Karen!"

"This is mercy!" said she.

And the organ played again, and the children's voices in the choir mingled sweetly with it. The bright sunbeams streamed warmly through the windows upon Karen's seat. Her heart was so full of sunshine, of peace and gladness, that it broke; her soul flew upon a sunbeam to her Father in heaven, where not a look of reproach awaited her, not a word was breathed of the red shoes.

ILLUSTRATOR
BIOGRAPHIES

Anne Anderson

Anne Anderson was born in Scotland in 1874. She spent her childhood in Argentina, where she became interested in illustration, before returning to Britain in her late twenties. In 1912, Anderson married Alan Wright. Wright was a painter who had previously been fairly successful, but whose commissions had dried up due to his association with a controversial Baron Corvo work he had illustrated in 1898. The two of them settled in Berkshire, and began to collaborate on a number of illustrated works.

Anderson was considered the driving force in the partnership, and her work quickly became extremely popular. Over the course of her life, she produced more than a hundred illustrated books, as well as etchings, watercolours and greeting cards.

Anderson's work has been compared to that of her contemporaries, such as Charles Robinson, Jessie M. King and Mabel Lucie Attwell. Here best-remembered illustrations are those she penned for works by Hans Christian Andersen and the Grimm Brothers. Anderson died in 1930, aged 56.

Honor C. Appleton

Honor C. Appleton was born in England in 1879. She started her illustrating career as a student of the Royal Academy Schools, and she went on to develop a distinctive and delicate watercolour style. Influenced by contemporary illustrators such as Arthur Rackham, Heath Robinson, Kate Greenaway and Annie French, Appleton illustrated over 150 books during the course of her career. Her most famous works are *Our Nursery Rhyme Book* (1912), Charles Perrault's *Fairy Tales* (1919) and Hans Christian Andersen's *Fairy Tales* (1922). Appleton died in 1951.

Maxwell Armfield

Maxwell Armfied was born in Ringwood, Hampshire, England in 1881. In 1887, he was admitted to the Birmingham School of Art – at that point under the headmastership of influential artist Edward R. Taylor – and was heavily influenced by the then-burgeoning Arts and Crafts Movement.

In 1902, Armfield left Birmingham for Paris, where he studied at the Académie de la Grande Chaumière. He exhibited at the Paris Salon in 1904, after which his painting *Faustine* was bought and donated to the National Museum of Luxembourg. Returning to London some years later, Armfield embarked on a series of one-man exhibitions, showing at the Robert Ross's Carfax Gallery, the Leicester Galleries and elsewhere.

Aside from painting, Armfield was a prolific illustrator and versatile decorative artist. He was also heavily involved in theatre, music, teaching and journalism, and wrote almost twenty books, including poetry, travelogues and textbooks. He died in 1972, aged 91..

Gordon Browne

Gordon Browne was born in Barnstead, Surrey, England in 1858. The son of notable illustrator Hablot Knight Browne (who as 'Phiz' illustrated books by Charles Dickens), he studied art at the Heatherley School of Fine Art and South Kensington Schools, and began to receive professional commissions before he graduated. Browne's first book illustrations appeared in Ascott R. Hope's short story 'The Day After the Holidays' (1875), and from the 1880s onwards he was one of Britain's most prolific illustrators, publishing work in newspapers, magazines and many books by children's authors. Amongst his best-remembered illustrations are those in the 1901 edition of *Fairy Tales from Hans Andersen*. Browne died in 1932, aged 74.

Andreas Duncan Carse

Andreas Duncan Carse was born in 1876 to parents of Scottish and Swedish descent. Not much is known about his upbringing and life in general aside from the fact that he was an accomplished artist and illustrator whose work has been enjoyed by generations.

He provided the illustrations for Lucy M. Scott's *Dewdrops from Fairyland* (1912), a collection of short stories originally entitled *Entirely Unaided* that was remarkably written by the author when she was just nine years old.

Carse also notably illustrated the 1912 addition of Hans Christian Andersen's *Fairy Tales*, a collection of over 200 stories that has been translated into more than 125 language since it's first publication. Despite being a prolific writer of plays, novels, travelogues, and poems, it was for the writing of this book that Andersen was most famous. It went through many editions over the years and, and is renowned for the variety of illustrators who have brought its stories to life over the years. Carse's contributions to *Fairy Tales* arguably solidified his reputation as an accomplished illustrator of children's books.

Carse is known to have exhibited his beautiful artwork at numerous events and locations, beginning with an exhibition at the *Royal Academy* in 1904. He exhibited under the auspices of the British Council at Biennale in 1912, and began displaying his work regularly at the *Royal Academy* between 1922 and 1938. the *Fine Art Society*, the *London Salon* and the *Walker Art Gallery* in Liverpool are all other locations known to have played host to Carse's work.

Besides canvases and the pages of children's books, Carse's work has adorned a variety of other surfaces. He designed paintings for the ceiling of the *Detroit Athletic Club* and, in 1933, his works *Birds of the Old World* and *Birds of the New World* were used by Cunard to decorate the dining rooms of its flagship liner, *The Queen Mary*.

Andreas Duncan Carse, father of the famous British explorer Duncan Carse, passed away in 1938.

Jennie Harbour

Jennie Harbour was born in approximately 1893, most likely in London, England. Despite the fact that she was a talented and popular illustrator, and her works are now collector's items, little is known about her life. During the twenties, Harbour worked for The Raphael Tuck Publishing Company, a renowned printer of popular books and illustrated postcards. A defining artist of the Art Deco era, her most famous work is probably *My Book of Favourite Fairy Tales* (1921), which featured twelve colour plates and numerous black and white illustrations. Harbour also illustrated editions of *Hans Andersen's Stories* and My Book Of *Mother Goose Nursery Rhymes*. She died during the fifties.

Kay Nielsen

Kay Rasmus Nielsen was born in Copenhagen, Denmark in 1886. Hailing from an artistic family – his father was a theatre director and his mother was one of the most celebrated actresses of her time – Nielsen studied art in Paris between 1904 and 1911, before moving to England. He received his first commission in 1913, providing 24 colour plates and more than 15 monotone illustrations for *In Powder and Crinoline, Fairy Tales Retold by Sir Arthur Quiller-Couch*.

A year later, in 1914, Nielsen contributed 25 colour plates and a number of monotone images to the Norwegian folk tale *East of the Sun and West of the Moon*. During World War I, Nielsen worked on stage design, before turning to illustrated books once more with the publication of *Fairy Tales by Hans Andersen* (1924), to which he contributed 12 colour plates and more than 40 monotone illustrations. Many view this as some of

Nielsen's best work. He followed it a year later with *Hansel and Gretel, and Other Stories by the Brothers Grimm.*

In 1939, Nielsen left for California, where he found work with The Walt Disney Company. Amongst other things, he designed the 'Night on Bald Mountain' sequence for the film classic *Fantasia.* However, Nielsen was let go in 1941, and the last decade or so of his life proved a difficult time, during which he struggled for paid work and eventually fell into poverty. Indeed, it wasn't until some time after his death in 1957, aged 71, that Nielsen came to be viewed as one of the notable figures of the 'golden age of illustration'.

Charles Robinson

Charles Robinson was born in Islington, London, England in 1870. The son of an illustrator, and the brother of famous illustrators Thomas Heath Robinson and William Heath Robinson, he served a seven-year apprenticeship as a printer and took art lessons in the evenings. In 1892, Robinson won a place at the Royal Academy, but was unable to take it up due to lack of finances.

It wasn't until the age of 25 that Robinson began to sell his work professionally. His first full book was Robert Louis Stevenson's *A Child's Garden of Verses* (1895). The work was very well-received, going through a number of print runs. Over the rest of his life, Robinson illustrated many more fairy tales and children's books, including Eugene Field's *Lullaby Land* (1897), W. E. Cule's *Child Voices* (1899), Friedrich de la Motte Fouqué's *Sintram and His Companions* (1900), *Alice's Adventures in Wonderland* (1907), *Grimm's Fairy Tales* (1910) and Frances Hodgson Burnett's *The Secret Garden* (1911).

Robinson was also an active painter, especially in later life, and was elected to the Royal Institute of Painters in Water Colours in 1932. He died in 1937, aged 67.

W. Heath Robinson

William Heath Robinson was born in North London, England in 1872. Hailing from an artistic family – his brothers Thomas Heath and Charles were both respected illustrators – he studied at both the Islington School of Art and the Painting Schools of the Royal Academy. Originally, Robinson wanted to make a living as a landscape painter, but by the age of 25 had switched his attentions to producing illustrations for the burgeoning printed publications of the day.

In 1897, Robinson began publishing his earliest book illustrations. In 1902, he had his first minor success with the popular children's book, *The Adventures of Uncle Lubin*. Two years, *Rabelais* was published, containing more than 250 of his black and white illustrations in the Art Nouveau style. This book launched Robinson's career, establishing him as a major and sought-after artist.

However, Robinson was still struggling for money – not least because the publisher of *Uncle Lubin* and *Rabelais* had gone bust before he got paid – and he turned to the most accessible source of immediate income he could find: humorous drawings for magazines such as *The Tattler, The Bystander* and *The Sketch*. Alongside this, Robinson continued to illustrate books, including editions of *Chaucher* (1905), *The Iliad* (1906) and *The Odyssey* (1906) – the three of which were amongst his first colour commissions.

Over the next few years, Robinson produced a number of the full-colour gift books for which he is well-remembered, including editions of *Twelfth Night* (1908), *The Collected Verse of Rudyard Kipling* (1909) and *Bill the Minder* (1912). He also continued to produce series of humorous drawings poking fun at ordinary living. Many of these featured highly complicated mechanical contraptions carrying out an extremely uncomplicated task with great effort – hence a "Heath Robinson" existing as a common idiom for complex inventions which produce absurdly simple results. The drawings were published in book form over a period of thirty years.

Robinson produced his autobiography, *My Life of Line,* in 1938. He died six years later, aged 72.

Dugald Stewart Walker

Dugald Stewart Walker was born in Richmond, Virginia, USA in 1883. He studied at the New York School of Design, and his first substantial illustrations appeared in the 1912 publication *Stories for Pictures*. In the foreword to that book, the author, Helen Mackay, described Walker as "a new artist of remarkable talent, suggesting Rackham and Dulac but entirely original in spirit and execution."

Two years later, one of his best-remembered and most heavily-illustrated works, *Fairy Tales from Hans Christian Andersen* (1914), was published. Over the following decade, many other commissions followed, including *Dream Boats and Other Stories* (1918); *The Wishing-Fairy's Animal Friends* (1921); *Rainbow Gold* (1922); *Snythergen* (1923); *The Six Who Were Left in a Shoe* (1923); *Many Wings* (1923); *Squiffer* (1924); *The Golden Porch* (1925); and *Orpheus with His Lute* (1926). Walker died in 1937, aged 54.

Helen Stratton

Helen Stratton was born in London, England in 1892. She began painting at a young age, but it was for her work as an illustrator that she would eventually become best-known. Strongly influenced by the Art Nouveau school of Glasgow, over the course of her career, Stratton illustrated at least five editions of Hans Christian Andersen's fairy tales, an edition of *Grimm's Fairy Tales* (1903), and *Stories from Andersen, Grimm and the Arabian Nights* (1929). She also painted watercolour illustrations for George MacDonald's *The Princess and the Goblin* and *The Princess and Curdie*. Stratton died in 1925, aged just 32.

Material in this book has been sourced from the following titles:

Edna F. Hart, Illustrator. *Hans Andersen's Fairy Tales - Vol. I.* 1885
Thomas, Charles, and William Robinson, Illustrators.
Fairy Tales from Hans Christian Andersen. 1899
Helen Stratton, Illustrator. *Fairy Tales of Hans Andersen.* 1899
Gordon Browne, Illustrator. *Fairy Tales from Hans Christian Andersen.* 1902
Maxwell Armfield, Illustrator. *Faery Tales from Hans Andersen.* 1910
A. Duncan Carse, Illustrator. *Hans Andersen's Fairy Tales.* 1912
W. Heath Robinson, Illustrator. *Hans Andersen's Fairy Tales.* 1913
Dugald Stewart Walker, Illustrator. *Fairy Tales from Hans Christian Andersen.* 1914
Honor C. Appleton, Illustrator. *Fairy Tales by Hans Christian Andersen.* 1922
Kay Nielsen, Illustrator. *Hans Andersen's Fairy Tales.* 1924
Anne Anderson, Illustrator. *The Hans Andersen's Fairy Tales, Part 1.* 1924
Jennie Harbour, Illustrator. *Hans Andersen's Stories.* 1932

Printed in Great Britain
by Amazon